Then he was spied in such a hurry
causing a seaside fuss and flurry.

Take care and do beware
there's rough and tumble down at the fair.

Such a kerfuffle
and what a to do,
Woof has pinched
six sizzling sausages
from off the barbeque.

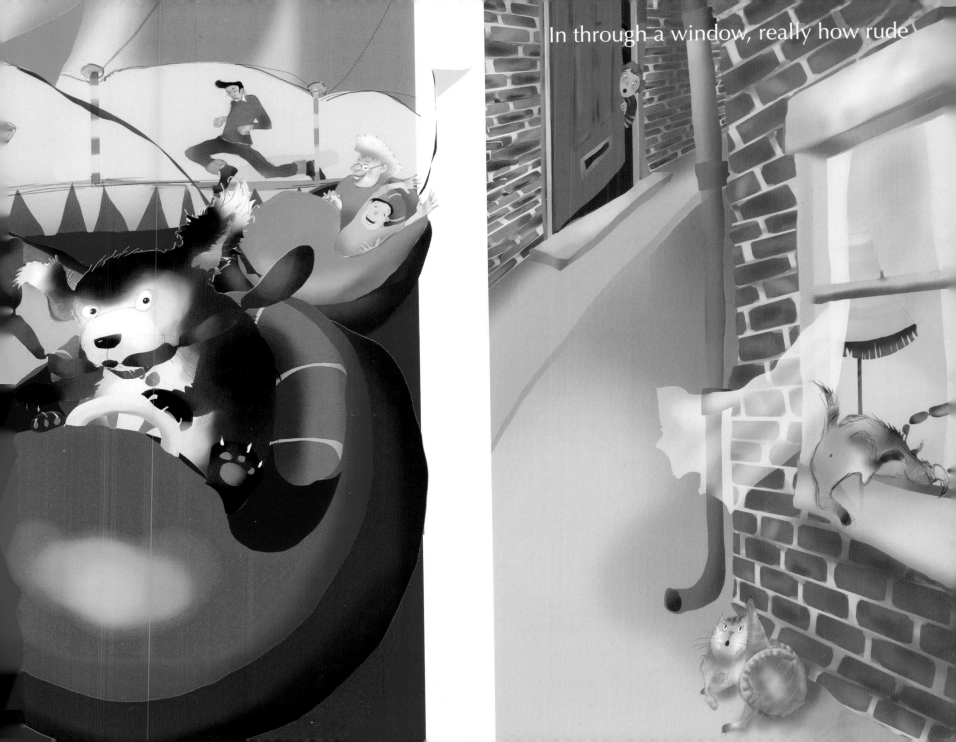

In through a window, really how rude

biscuits go everywhere still unchewed.

Dafter and dafter more people chase after into the classroom our naughty dog zooms.

The ferry boat has left without
soggy cyclists who shout,
yet on and on Woof will dash
leaving them to splosh and splash

DELAYS

It's always a jostle on the Metro train
he's on, then he's off again.

In the library it should be quiet,
but Woof and his antics are causing a riot.

Hear those vexed and angry calls,
it's confusion on the market stalls.

The chase went on for miles and miles
but our faces are all smiles
because what ever can we see
six puppies shall have sausages for tea.